From Shad Helmstetter, Ph.D.

The Incredible Adventures of
Shadrack the Self-Talk Bear™

BOOK 1 — *The Story of Planet Excellence*

The first book in the Shadrack series begins on the planet Excellence, the home of Shadrack and the Self-Esteem Team, who fight to save their planet from the terrible Negatroids.

BOOK 2 — *The Incredibears on Planet Earth*

Shadrack and the Self-Esteem Team travel to planet Earth to save the children, and confront the Negatroids in a giant amusement park filled with thousands of terrified Earth kids.

BOOK 3 — *The Rise of the Great Bear*

Shadrack, unarmed and alone, is forced to face the evil Negatroids who want to destroy him, when help arrives in the form of a mysterious bear with amazing powers.

Powerful, positive messages for children of all ages, from the world's leading authority on Positive Self-Talk.

Shad Helmstetter, Ph.D., is the pioneering dean of self-talk. He is the best-selling author of more than twenty books for grownups. In the remarkable Shadrack the Self-Talk Bear series, Dr. Helmstetter brings his life-changing message of self-talk to children of all ages.

www.shadhelmstetter.com

Listen to special self-talk for kids and adults from Dr. Shad Helmstetter

Self-Talk for Kids

Featuring Shadrack the Bear

Self-Talk for Older Kids

Self-Talk for Adults

Stream the top self-talk audio programs direct to your listening device.

www.SelfTalkPlus.com

www.SelfTalkPlus.com

The Incredible Adventures of

Shadrack the Self-Talk™ Bear

Book 1

For Children of all Ages

The Story of Planet
Excellence

Shad Helmstetter, Ph.D.

The Incredible Adventures of
Shadrack the Self-Talk Bear

Book I

The Story of Planet Excellence

Published by Park Avenue Press
362 Gulf Breeze Pkwy., #104
Gulf Breeze, FL 32561

Helmstetter, Shad
The Incredible Adventures of Shadrack the Self-Talk Bear
Book I
The Story of Planet Excellence

ISBN 978-0-9970861-4-0 (*Printed format*)
ISBN 978-0-9970861-5-7   (*Digital format*)

For more information:
www.shadhelmstetter.com

Chapter One

Planet Excellence

If you look up into the northern sky on a clear night, you will see a group of stars that looks like a giant pot, or a big dipper in the sky. That group of stars is in the constellation Ursa Major, which means 'The Great Bear.'

Circling around one of the stars in Ursa Major there is a small blue, white, and green planet. It is the planet Excellence, the home of Shadrack the Bear.

This is the story of something that came to the planet Excellence from somewhere far off in space. It was something so frightening and so dangerous that it threatened the very existence of Excellence itself. What happened *there,* on the planet Excellence, is why Shadrack is *here* with us now, on the planet Earth.

*   *   *   *   *   *   *

For most of its history, the planet Excellence was a very friendly and peaceful planet. It was always the home of the Bears of Excellence. There were brown bears and black bears and golden bears and white bears and bears of every kind and description living there, and all of them lived together on the planet in peace.

The bears ruled the land and the seas and even the skies of Excellence. But they took care of their planet, and it was a beautiful place to live. After many years, the bears of Excellence had also become very intelligent. They had learned how to make schools and homes and places to work. It was a perfect place to live and dream, and make any good dream come true.

On the planet Excellence, every bear mattered. Every bear was important. Not a single dream or good idea went unnoticed. Any bear of any age, with any idea, would be listened to. Even very young bears who thought new ideas about anything would be heard. And because of the idea of always listening to new ideas, the bears of Excellence had learned to *excel*.

Because of their remarkable ability to listen to new ideas, the bears of Excellence had also created concepts and ideas that were almost unimaginable. They learned to live lives of life-long health, unstoppable attitude, and a strength of self that had never been known before the coming of the Great Bear.

Along with making their planet work, the bears of Excellence created many wonderful things. Music from little devices they could carry in a pocket. Pictures and sound from three-dimensional holovision they could watch in their homes. 'Touch-Point Artistry' that allowed any little bear or older bear to create pictures and stories, just by touching a 'Think Screen,' and watching the ideas in their mind come to life on the screen.

To describe Excellence perfectly, you would almost have to decide which time of which day to describe it, because the bears of Excellence had also learned how to change the color of their skies. There were bright crimson and orange skies for creativity, golden skies for wisdom and learning, aqua blue and emerald green skies for health and healing, and soft pink skies for rest and calmness of spirit.

And then, of course, there were the celebration skies, those wonderful times when all the bears of Excellence would celebrate some wonderful happening. They celebrated births and weddings and winning rolley tournaments, school graduations, the turn of the seasons, any bear doing something especially good, kayak and swimming races, important birthdays . . . almost anything at all.

On the planet Excellence, there were twelve big events that were celebrated every year. Each of those events would light up the skies with great bursts of fireworks and beautiful nighttime pyrotechnic displays that never ceased to create awe and wonder in the bears of Excellence.

But the biggest of all the events, one that would literally *fill* the skies of Excellence with brilliant, colorful fireworks, was the commemoration of the arrival of the Great Bear and the birth of Excellence itself.

On those wonderful and joyous occasions, each year the skies above Excellence would be filled with a magnificent nighttime canopy of exploding skyrockets of every possible color. The thundering noise of the rockets and their shimmering cascades of dazzling lighted 'messages of positive' never failed to send shivers of excitement down the backs of every little bear and every big bear on Excellence.

Because the bears of Excellence had learned to live without wars, the frequent and beautiful, magnificent bursts of exploding fireworks in their nighttime skies—for one celebration or another—was the only use they ever had of anything that even remotely resembled the explosive weapons of war.

The bears of Excellence had also created wonderful bearplanes to fly in the sky. And they had even learned how to build starships that would take them into the deep dark space beyond the constellation Ursa Major.

The bears of Excellence slept well each night, knowing that they lived in a world of peace, security, unstoppable personal growth, and unlimited possibilities.

In all of the known universe, there was no better place to live, grow, and excel than the planet Excellence. None of the bears doubted that their idyllic life would go on forever. And none of them could even have imagined that the beautiful world of Excellence was about to change.

Chapter Two

Shadrack the Bear

Shadrack the Bear had lived on Excellence all his life. He was still a youthbear, but a lot of times he thought more like an olderbear. Shadrack was like the other bears on Excellence in most ways, but in some ways he was different—in a good kind of way.

For one thing, even as a youthbear, Shadrack liked to think a lot, almost as much as some of the teacherbears. And his favorite way to think was while he was looking at the stars in the night sky above Excellence. All the bears liked to look at the stars now and then, but for Shadrack, looking at stars was something he could do for hours on end. The nighttime sky over Excellence was ablaze with light from a million stars, and Shadrack would sit on a quiet hillside all by himself and imagine what it was like out there, far out in the deepest parts of space.

When Shadrack wasn't watching the night skies and thinking about space and other grownup thoughts, he seemed kind of normal. He liked to play rolley with his friends, and he was very good at the game and his team was a winning team. But he also liked it when the other bears won, and he would often spend as much time encouraging the *other* team as he would spend trying to help his own team win.

When Shadrack was spending time with his friends—bears like Wheely, Holly, Marathon, Theo, Poppy, Scuba, and Believer Bear—he got along great with all of them. But there were also times when it was clear that he thought 'different' than the way his friends thought.

Instead of just playing a game, Shadrack wanted to know *why* the game was fun to play. Instead of just noticing that some bears could do something especially well, he wanted to know *how* they got good at it. Instead of just watching a starship take off from Excellence to travel to someplace in space, Shadrack wanted to know *where* it was going, and *why*, and *what* they would find when they got there.

It was because of Shadrack's special kind of thinking, and always wanting to figure things out, and always wanting to help other bears do their best, that he would end up playing an important role in the story of planet Excellence—and in the story of the terrible Negatroids who came to destroy it.

Chapter Three

The Terrible Negatroids

It was when one of the planet's starships returned to Excellence after a long journey out into the stars, that the trouble on Excellence began.

When the starship returned to the friendly blue and aqua and pink and golden skies of Excellence, the crewbears did not notice that something from far off space had followed them home. And it was something very bad.

Far in the distance behind the golden starship, as it had made its way home, was a large, dark, cloud-like form, a shroud of haze so dark that it could scarcely be seen in the darkness of space. If one were to have watched it closely, it would have been noticed that the distant cloud of darkness would blot out the stars behind it. But none of the bears on the starship was looking for it. And no one noticed, so no one knew it was there.

The crewbears of the starship were welcomed home as heroes, and all of planet Excellence watched and listened eagerly as the explorers told of their travels and discoveries in distant space. For days on end, the bears of Excellence talked of nothing else.

They were so busy celebrating that they didn't notice when some days the skies over Excellence did not seem to be as bright as they usually were. It was like a shadow was spreading itself over the entire planet, and making it darker.

Also, even as unusual as it was on Excellence, no one noticed at first when a few of the youngerbears and kidbears began acting strangely. First it was nothing really, just one or two youngerbears fighting in school. The bears of Excellence had learned not to fight, so no one paid attention when it first happened, because they thought the bears were only playing. But they weren't playing. They were *fighting*.

Then a few of the parentbears noticed that their kidbears were acting strangely at home and on the sports fields. The younger bears got angry for no reason at all, and yelled at grown-ups, or sat sullenly in front of the holovision, looking unhappy. Normally fun and exciting sporting events like bearball and rolley turned into fights on the field.

Within days after the time the explorer bears had returned home from their far-off journey in space, it was clear that something was wrong. The kidbears of the planet Excellence were changing. And as time went on, things got worse—much worse. Within a few short weeks they were turning into angry, unhappy, fighting little bears, not like bears of Excellence at all.

Strange new words that had not been spoken or heard on Excellence since the days of the planet's earliest and once barbaric history, were suddenly being heard in classrooms and playgrounds, and even in kidbears' bedrooms and living rooms. Words like *selfish*, and *stupid*, and *hate*, and *clumsy*, erupted into kidbears' vocabularies like poisonous vapors boiling from a pot of venomous verbal stew. Suddenly the angry, fight-like new words were everywhere in the air.

They were heard on playgrounds where angry and hurtful words hadn't been heard before. They were heard in classrooms where only words of learning had been heard before. They were heard in homes where only words of love and understanding and guidance had been heard before.

And it wasn't just the *words* of the kidbears that were changing. It was the *thinking* that went on in the heads of the kidbears themselves. One young bear would yell at another, *"You're so stupid! You can't do anything right!"* The other bear would yell back, *"I'm* stupid? . . . *No, you're stupid!"* And with the words came thoughts that would make both of them feel a new kind of pain.

Kidbears who had never ever before felt stupid or slow or clumsy or not smart enough or not good enough, suddenly felt all of those things.

And the more they heard the words said to them, and the more they shouted the same kinds of things back, the worse they felt. And the stupider and slower, and clumsier, or not smart enough, or not good enough they started to become.

In time, the older bears began to realize that something wasn't right. The more they noticed, the more they asked other olderbears if they, too, had noticed something was wrong.

But by the time most of the olderbears recognized how completely the new words were taking over the lives and the minds of the kidbears of Excellence, the *change of mind* had begun. And the change of mind, once the olderbears realized it was happening, was more frightening than anything they had ever imagined.

Like a cloud of darkness spreading over the land, the first cloud of unhappiness and fights and anger and selfishness and littlebear bitterness was spreading over Excellence.

A blanket of grayness turned the afternoon sky from brilliant blue or fiery crimson to a deep pressing haze of bleakness. Like the dark cloud of 'something' that had followed silently behind the space voyagers from Excellence when they had returned home to their planet. Like that ominous cloud of darkness that had blotted out the distant stars as it passed, a cloak of eerie, malevolent darkness now pulled itself tighter and tighter around the planet Excellence.

As the cloud wrapped itself closer to its prey, the young bears of Excellence were sadly, but clearly, changing.

The cloud of darkness and the angry turmoil of despair it brought with it began to pull the life out of the kidbears and youngerbears of Excellence, like an evil demon squeezing the life out of a helpless teddy bear. The Terrible Negatroids had arrived, and they had come to destroy the children of Excellence, and the once-promising future of the planet Excellence itself.

*   *   *   *   *   *   *

Shadrack had first seen the change in the sky on one of the nights he was sitting alone on the hillside watching the stars and thinking. He had seen something, ever so faint, like shadows of dark misty clouds, crossing the sky above him. And it was something he had never seen before. The dark wisps of clouds were moving, not like other clouds, but like clouds that were alive, and moving strangely, decisively, like they knew where they were going.

The next night he had seen them again, larger, darker, and closer this time. Each night, as he watched the strange, moving ghost-like shades of darkness that were covering more and more stars with blackness, Shadrack became more and more uneasy.

As he watched the darkness covering the stars, he felt a tightening in his stomach that wouldn't go away. This didn't look right. This was something very new, and Shadrack felt, something very *wrong*.

It was when the kidbears on Excellence started to change from good to bad, that Shadrack realized that the change in the kidbears had begun just after he had first seen the unnatural dark wisps of clouds darkening the sky. And when he realized that, he saw what it meant: the *darkness* was causing the *badness*.

That was when Shadrack decided to talk to old Eli Bear, the oldest, wisest bear on Excellence, and tell him what he had seen, and what he believed was happening.

When Shadrack talked to the wise old bear, Eli listened, and he did not doubt the younger bear's message; he seemed to understand completely. As he questioned Shadrack, wanting to know more, the old bear did not look doubtful; he looked worried.

Within the same hour that Shadrack had brought his message to him, old Eli had called for an emergency meeting of all of the olderbears of Excellence.

It was when Shadrack had used his best thinking and had started to figure out what was wrong on planet Excellence, and where the plague of badness might be coming from, that his future would change forever.

Chapter Four

Emergency on Excellence

As soon as old Eli summoned them, the olderbears and elderbears of Excellence began to gather in Great Hall, where they had often come together to discuss important things.

Great Hall was a giant, auditorium-like cavern with rows and rows of seats, and a big stage area at the front, with long tables where the elderbears sat. Right in the center of the stage was a special chair that was taller than all the rest. This was the special seat of the most important and wisest bear of all.

One time, many years ago, this had been the chair where the wise and powerful Great Bear had sat. But the Great Bear had been gone for many years, and now, in his place, sat another very elderbear, the wisest bear now on Excellence, wonderful old Eli Bear.

After the olderbears and the elderbears took their seats in Great Hall, Eli Bear asked the assembly if they had witnessed the scourge of darkness that was sweeping across Excellence. He would wait to tell them his own frightening conclusions until after he had heard what the other bears had to say.

"Bears of Excellence," the well-respected bear named Sazza began, clearing her throat and waiting for silence to make its way through the cavernous spaces of Great Hall. "I fear that a great plague of evil has come to our beloved world.

"Something is destroying our children. Something we cannot see is stealing their minds and their spirits from them, and turning them into bears that fight and quarrel . . . and growl and snarl and tear at one another like the bears that fought here a long time ago. Something is taking their spirits from them," Sazza Bear continued.

"Something is trying to turn our precious, beautiful, positive-minded youngerbears back into the wild bears that once lived here. Something bad is turning the children of Excellence into nothing more than the pathetic beasts of the forests of our own past, who could do nothing more than forage for food and fight each other for survival."

"She's right!" shouted out Micah bear, himself the proud father of two handsome youngerbears. "Only yesterday, I saw something I thought I would never see," he continued. "I saw *blood*," Micah said, his face showing the horror of his feelings at saying the word. "I saw three youngerbears striking another bear until the poor little thing fell to the ground, battered and bleeding."

"And *I* saw two gangs of youngerbears fighting each other in the streets, with sticks and rocks," said another olderbear, slowly shaking his head both in sorrow and disbelief. "Something is terribly wrong here," he said to the others.

Then another parentbear spoke out. "And have you noticed the look in some of our kidbears' eyes?" she asked. "It is as though someone has taken the light out of them. It is like the bright and wonderful spirit of Excellence has been taken away from them. They just look at you as though they aren't even seeing you at all."

All of the other bears nodded their once happy bearheads in sadness.

"We worked so long and so hard to be civilized," said one of the Elderbears who were present in the hall. "We learned how to live in peace, and how to think in positive and worthwhile ways. We learned how to make wonderful, caring schools and truly brilliant universities and amazing science and art and music, and how to live together without wars or fighting," he said.

"Many years ago, when our ancestors lived in the rocks and the forests, their caves were nothing more than burrows where they slept away their winters or hid from other bears. Now our homes are happy homes, filled with learning and laughter and light. At least they were until now," he said, a tear showing in the corner of one great bear eye. "It doesn't feel like Excellence anymore."

One by one, the parentbears and olderbears told their stories of what was happening to Excellence. One by one, they told of their fruitless struggle to help their youngerbears, or protect them from their new and frightening ways.

And each of them, in some way, expressed the same deep worry—that soon, if something did not change, Excellence would not be Excellence anymore. And the beautiful youngerbears, with their wonderful futures in front of them, would be no more. If something was not done to help them now, soon there would be no "Excellence" at all!

Finally, after all of the bears had been given a chance to be heard, a hush began to fall over the hall. It was time for old Eli to speak.

The wisest of all of the bears of Excellence was seated at his special place in the higher chair, watching all of them with great knowing and understanding. And when silence finally filled the great cavern, old Eli spoke.

"My dear, dear bears of Excellence," he began, "we have an emergency. One that threatens the very existence of Excellence itself.

"To tell you what has happened, I will begin with a story that you must hear. It is a story I am deeply saddened to have to share with you."

And then, after a very long pause, Eli said, "I believe I know what has come to Excellence. It has been here before, in our long, distant past, and I believe it has returned."

When Eli spoke these words, every ear in Great Hall was turned to him. Not a single other bear said anything at all, or even breathed too loudly.

Eli continued, "As all of you know, I am the only Elderbear remaining who actually sat at the feet of the Great Bear. That was many years ago. Before the Great Bear went to his final summer, he gave me a very important, but very secret, message. He said that it was a message that I must keep to myself, and tell no one, until the right time had come.

"I had always wondered if the incredible secret the Great Bear told me was only a myth," Eli continued. "That is, until now. Now I believe that what he told me was as true as the birth of Excellence itself. I have kept this secret for many long years, and during that time, I have told no one. But now it is time to tell you the secret that the Great Bear left with me."

With that, if the bears in the Great Hall had been listening closely before, they were now leaning forward in their seats to hear even better. There was not a single sound in the great cavern when Eli began to speak again.

Chapter Five

The Planet *Average*

"As you know, many years ago," Eli began, "long before there was a planet called Excellence, our planet had a different name. It was called the planet *Average*. And it was, at its best, 'average,' and usually worse.

"On the planet Average, there lived only wild bears of the forest—your ancestors. But they did not live here alone. There were birds and other animals, of course, but there was something else living here, too. Something evil. Something dark and destructive. And it was this dark, fearsome thing that kept your ancestor bears in the forest for so long. Not only did this dark thing *live* here," Eli said, and then his voice lowered to the quietest of whispers, ". . . it *ruled* here."

Eli paused just a moment to let what he was saying to them sink in, and then he continued. "The darkness that once ruled this planet was not a single beast of any kind. It was many of them. And it was not bears or animals. It was," and here Eli paused again, ". . . *it was the terrible Negatroids.*

"The Negatroids lived here long ago. And now they have returned," Eli said, his strong, clear elderly bear voice filled with a strength of emotion seldom heard, especially from Eli himself. "They have followed our own starship back to Excellence from far off in space, and that is very bad, indeed.

"The Negatroids are a race of beings that live in shadows. They are shades of darkness, shadowy ghost-like beings that are scarcely seen. But what they *do* can be seen everywhere.

"The Negatroids can disguise themselves as angry parents, or bad-tempered teachers in school, bullies on the playground, friends who aren't really 'friends,' and even newscasters on the holovision who tell us only bad news.

"We all know that the bears of Excellence have lived in happiness because we have learned that our words and our thoughts form and shape everything about our lives. We know that every word we speak to our kidbears becomes a part of who they are and who they will become. And we know that every word counts.

"The Negatroids know this, too. That is why they attack our kidbears and youngerbears with *words*, the worst kinds of words and thoughts, the worst kinds of messages possible for our little bears' young, open minds.

"So far," Eli continued, "The Negatroids have chosen to attack our children one by one, whispering negative words and thoughts into their ears, and changing their minds from good to bad. We have all seen what that is doing to our children.

"But they can do even worse. The terrible Negatroids have the strength to attack our planet Excellence 'en masse,' all at once. They are able to cover our once peaceful planet Excellence with a storm of negative thoughts and ideas so powerful and so harmful and deadly, that even the beautiful flowers in our gardens will wither and die, and even the strongest of our bears will bow their heads in defeat and despair.

"Hear this," Eli said, choosing his words carefully. "It is the goal of the Negatroids to *steal the minds and souls of our youngerbears.* And steal them, they will.

"They take our little bears' minds and they pull the beliefs and futures, and their dreams and their lives right *out* of them. And in the place of all the good and wonderful things we have worked so hard to teach our little bears, the Negatroids fill their minds with fear and hatred and disbelief and failure.

"When that happens," old Eli said very sadly, shaking his wizened old head slowly, "the Negatroids capture our little bears' *spirits.*

"And when they steal them, they freeze each little spirit in the space that surrounds our planet, in a place called *'The Nozone Layer.'* And unless we do something now, our little bears' spirits will remain there, frozen in the darkness of the Nozone, forever.

"That, my dear bears, is what is happening now. *We are losing the children of Excellence* to the negative words and thoughts of the terrible Negatroids!"

Suddenly, the mass of the bears in the great cavern was not quiet at all. Suddenly, Great Hall was filled with shouts and questions, and bewilderment and confusion.

And now, for the first time any of them could ever remember, there was something else in the great room with them. Something that none of the bears living on Excellence had ever quite known. Suddenly, making its way through the room and through the bears that were gathered there, was something called *"fear."*

But above the talking and the questions and the confusion and fear, Eli's clear voice was the strongest. "There is more!" he said, his voice ringing out over the assembly of bears. And with that, once again the bears fell silent, waiting for Eli to speak.

"For many years of its history, our planet lived under the rule of the terrible Negatroids," Eli went on. "All of its wars, all of its fighting were caused by the evil beings. Their words of hate and despair were everywhere. Every youngerbear was surrounded by them, and filled with them.

"The Negatroids were relentless in taking the little bear thoughts and minds and spirits away from them. They whispered words of disbelief, and fear, and dissension, and disruption into their ears and into their minds.

"They took out the good, and put in the bad. They turned bear against bear, brown bear against white bear, golden bear against black bear, and made them fight each other instead of love each other. And as the bears grew older, their once beautiful minds were replaced by something dark, and nothing at all like the wonderful young bears they once were. And sadly, so our history was formed.

"But we were fortunate. Something happened that would change our history. Somehow, sent to us as a gift, a special bear arose on the planet. This bear was stronger than the rest. This special bear did not hear the words of the Negatroids. Instead of fighting his fellow bears, he fought the Negatroids. This special bear, as each of you knows, was the Great Bear.

"In time, the Great Bear taught the other bears how to fight back. Over many years of our history, it was this one bear who led us away from the fear and the fighting of the Negatroids, and out of the forests, and into the lives that we have today—into the world of Excellence.

"In our history books, this scourge of the terrible Negatroids has always been called 'The Enemy.' It was an enemy that was seldom seen, it was fought for years, and it was finally beaten. And since that time, until today, the name of that enemy has seldom even been spoken. Even the terrible name 'Negatroid' was all but erased from our language. All that remains of it is our own word for 'emptiness' or 'unhappiness.' The word, of course, is the word *negative.* And here on Excellence, even that word has been almost forgotten.

"But now," Eli said, "that word has come back. And far worse, the bringers of that word have returned. The Negatroids have once again come to the planet Excellence."

Then old Eli stood before the multitude of bears and held one bear paw high in the air. In his paw, Eli held something that every bear in the hall looked upon as Eli said his next words.

"I hold here a message from the Great Bear," Eli said. "In this scroll, I have the message and the counsel that the Great Bear passed down to us. As he taught us, *if you want to succeed, you must have a goal and a plan.* If we follow the plan the Great Bear has given us, together, with his guidance, we may all save Excellence."

Eli then carefully opened the scroll and rolled it out, to let the other bears see the words that were written on it.

And sure enough, there were the words of the Great Bear himself. From where they were seated, the bears in attendance couldn't read all of the words, but they could see that this was truly an ancient message from the Great Bear.

It was a *plan*. Because of old Eli, and especially because of the ancient words of the Great Bear, the bears of Excellence had a plan! If they wanted to save the planet Excellence, there was something they could do.

Much later, as the olderbears and the elderbears of Excellence left their meeting that night, several of them stopped for a minute or two, and looked up . . . as though they could see something there, something dark and shadowy in the sky, a midnight mask, covering, one by one, each of the three moons above them.

But the other bears turned away, lost in their own thoughts and concerns about the kidbears and youngerbears of Excellence, worried and fearful about the Negatroids that had come to steal their children's minds. They were especially thinking about the plan that old Eli had revealed to them—a plan that may have come not a moment too soon.

Less than an hour after the olderbears had left Great Hall, Shadrack who was sitting on the hillside watching the sky, saw that the moons of Excellence could not be seen at all.

By now, all three of the moons were completely gone, blotted out by the cloud of darkness that silently descended through the night above him. In a sky that should have been filled with a million diamond-bright stars, there was not a star to be seen. The sky over Excellence was filled with nothing but a deep, endless darkness.

Chapter Six

The Evil *Low* and *No*

Even as the bears of Excellence had been learning about the terrible Negatroids, far above them, visible only by its appearance as an ominous, threatening cloud, the dark ship *Neanderthal I* hovered silently. Inside the ship, the two powerful leaders of the Negatroids planned their next step in their assault on the planet Excellence.

The leaders of the Negatroids were the two evil brothers named *"Low"* and *"No."* They were named for their disbelief in anything good or caring for anyone, and they were fighting with each other now, as they always did.

No wanted to send in all of the Negaforce troops at once, overwhelming the bears below with negative energy of an unprecedented strength.

Low wanted to continue to send their forces in slowly, breaking down the resistance of the bears of Excellence day by day as they had already started doing, negative word by negative word.

In the great spaceship *Neanderthal I,* its two large captain's chairs were empty. Instead of sitting, the two captains were both standing—or floating. None of the Negatroids really stood. They were too ghost-like and too shadow-like to really stand.

Now, the two leaders of the Universal Force of Negatroids known as the *Negaforce* glared at each other across the flickering lights of the control room's computer panel, as though they were the enemies of only each other.

"*I* say we destroy their minds with darkness and hatred and loathing and fear, all in one grand and glorious attack!" growled the infamous Negatroid leader No.

"And *I* say we destroy them *slowly*, one little bear mind at a time," his evil brother Low hissed back at him.

"Let us continue to steal their minds, destroy their self-esteem, break their little bear families apart, wreck their schools, and force them to believe in failure and darkness! Let us continue to take their little bear spirits from them. Let us teach them that hope is for the weak, that life is an unrewarding struggle, and that all good things lead to something bad."

"You like to destroy the little ones with words and thoughts that fill their minds with negative thoughts, so they have problems, fight each other, feel unfulfilled, and have miserable lives," No hissed back at his evil brother Low.

"I admit, all of that works," he said. "It destroys them and steals their spirits from them. But all that takes *time*. Why not just descend on them all at once, smother their precious little planet with the darkness of total negativity, and attack their cities with our most frightening weapon—*The Giant Voice of Doom?*"

As he said this, No's thin, glowing slits of eyes glowed a little brighter, and the two dark, horn-shaped appendages that formed the upper sides of the ghostly shadow of his head seemed to get sharper and more menacing.

"Don't you remember how completely we destroyed the brains of the ones whose self-esteem we took away?" Low's snake-like voice hissed sharply back at the shadowy form of his brother.

"We have always been at our best when we have whispered the worst of our thoughts into their open little minds. By doing that, we have taught children to lose all belief in themselves. And then we have taught them to turn on each other with ignorance, selfishness, bullying, cowardice, intimidation, and a complete lack of belief in anything good," Low breathed, his two slits of eyes glowing yellow-green as he said the words.

"That is the best way to destroy a planet completely," he concluded, confident of another success soon to be played out below them on the planet Excellence. "And that way they suffer *more*, and suffer *longer*."

Finally, No gave in to Low's strategy to continue to destroy the little bears of Excellence one by one. "Then let us double our efforts and increase our war of whispered words," No said. We will destroy their little bear minds, *steal their spirits,* and change their hearts slowly—but forever.

"However," No continued, "if we cannot destroy Excellence by stealing the minds and the spirits of their children as we are doing now, we must be prepared to take even greater, darker, measures. After all, the bears of Excellence have been taught to be positive and to have strong minds, and they have the will to excel."

"Don't worry," Low said to his brother, for the moment the snarl in his voice turning into something that sounded almost like joyous anticipation, something a Negatroid could never truly experience. "Whether we take their spirits slowly, or smother them in the darkness of an all-out attack, we *will* take them."

And with that, the dark gray spaceship *Neanderthal I*, with its armada of Negatroid warships trailing behind it, swooped down closer to the surface of Excellence, descending toward the twinkling lights of the landscape far below.

Chapter Seven

The War of the Words

To the bears of Excellence, it looked as though this year, Great Bear Day, with the wonderful celebration that had been planned to go along with it, now only days away, would not be the joyous celebration it usually was. With the Negatroids surrounding them, there might not be a Great Bear Day at all. What if the bears couldn't stop the Negatroids? What would happen then?

For one thing, the terrible Negatroids had unusual powers. Not only were they usually invisible, but they could pass through solid objects, just like a ghost. Only they weren't ghosts, they were real. Also, when they spoke, they could speak so only children—kidbears and youngerbears—could hear them. So they could say anything at all to children, and no parentbear or olderbear would even know that a Negatroid was around, or what it was saying.

Perhaps worst of all, Negatroids could disguise themselves as parents, teachers, and friends, and even newscasters reading negative news stories on the Holovision set, so the youngerbears would never know who was really talking to them.

Sometimes something that *looked* like an olderbear, who was supposed to love them, would do things or say things to them that would be *hurtful*. It wouldn't be a *real* olderbear or friendbear at all, of course. It would be a Negatroid who just *looked* like the olderbear who loved them or the friend who would help them. But with Negatroids, there was never any love or help at all. Just the opposite.

Sometimes a parentbear would yell at a kidbear, or use the worst kind of words, or suddenly become violent or angry. That too, would be a Negatroid, and not a *real* parent.

Sometimes a teacherbear would criticize or shame a little bear in front of the other kidbears, and make them believe that they were stupid or silly or not as good as someone else. That too, would be a Negatroid, and not a *real* teacher.

Sometimes another youngerbear would tempt its friends to do something wrong, or mean, or harmful, or self-destructive. And that, too, would be a Negatroid, and not a *real* friend.

Negatroids were best at whispering words into little kidbears' ears that would make them think and believe all the wrong things. And while they filled up the little kidbears' minds with all the *wrong* things, the Negatroids took out all the *good* things.

By putting the wrong words into the little bears' minds, the Negatroids took away the kidbears' self-esteem—they took away everything that made a kidbear good.

They took away the kidbears' wonderful and healthy *love* for themselves—and made them not able to love anyone else.

They took away their *trust* in themselves—and made them so they wouldn't trust others.

They took away their *belief* in themselves—and made them doubt everything they did.

They took away their *confidence*—and made them be afraid to do what was right.

They took away their wanting to *try*—and made them want to quit, or give up, or not even start at all.

They took away their determination to tell the *truth*—and replaced it with a willingness to tell a lie instead.

They took away their *friendliness*—and made them want to quarrel and fight.

They took away their *helpfulness* and *sharing*—and made them selfish and thinking only of themselves.

They took away their *positiveness*—and made them afraid to believe in anything good.

They took away their *hope*—and made them believe that nothing, for them, would ever get better.

When the Negatroids stole the *self-esteem* from the little bears of Excellence, when they took away the good things in their minds, they took away their *future*.

And the Negatroids did all of that with **words!**

"You're not good enough," they would whisper almost silently into some unsuspecting little bear's ear. *"You'll never amount to anything,"* they would say clearly and repeatedly to another little bear. *"You're so stupid,"* another bear would be told, again and again. The litany of negatives from the Negatroids was endless:

Can't you do anything right?
You're so clumsy!
When will you ever learn?

Why can't you be more responsible?
You're lazy!
You never tell the truth!
You never listen!
Why should I believe you?
You're just no good!
All you ever do is complain.
Your room is always a mess!
Who do you think you are?
You just don't try!
All you ever do is argue.
You think you're so smart!
You never care about anyone but yourself!
I'll tell you what's wrong with you . . .

. . . and *on, and on, and on.*

No *real* parentbear who loved their kidbears would ever say anything that would make them feel that unloved.

No *real* teacherbear who wanted to teach them would ever say something that would make them feel stupid, or unable to learn.

No *real* friendbear would ever say something that would hurt them. If anyone ever said anything like those kinds of things, it *had* to be a *Negatroid*.

And so the Negatroids waged their war of words. They whispered words, and shouted words, and repeated the negative words over and over, and talked and talked, and taunted and taunted.

And word by word, they were winning.

Chapter Eight

The Nozone

Eli had also told the assembly of olderbears something that had made even the bravest of them shudder with a sudden chill.

"When the Negatroids steal our little ones' spirits and their self-esteem," he told them, "you must also know what they do with them." Then Eli had looked at them straight on, as though he were telling them something that could be very bad.

"They take our kidbears' spirits to a place called the *Nozone layer*," Eli said, with a shudder himself. As old Eli told them about this dreadful place called the Nozone, the bears of Excellence could hardly believe that something this terrible could happen to their children.

Eli had heard of the Nozone many years before, but even his face had darkened when he read the words the Great Bear had given him. The Nozone was indeed a very unhappy place—if you could even call it a place at all.

In the thin atmosphere high above the planet Excellence, just at the place where the air is too thin to breath, and where space begins, the Negatroids had created a nearly invisible, vaporous cloud. And in that cloud, frozen for all eternity, were the silent little spirits of the kidbears whose minds had been stolen by the Negatroids.

If Eli and the other bears could not rescue them, their children's spirits would stay there, huddled together, silently shivering, without love or warmth, frozen in the unhappy space of the Nozone layer forever.

Without a spirit, the hapless littlebear kids themselves on the planet below would become one of the "*Uns*," the troubled kidbears who now lived in the streets, searching for their spirit, and never being able to find it.

"The Negatroids steal our children's self-esteem, and freeze their spirits far above the planet, in the Nozone," Eli told them. And then, one by one, our kidbears become the unhappy *Uns*.

If we cannot help our little ones get their true selves back again, we will lose them for good. And if we do not stop the Negatroids, they will destroy all of the kidbears of the planet Excellence. If the Negatroids win," Eli said very sadly, "we will lose Excellence forever.

"How many of our kidbears do we want to become one of the *Uns*?" Eli asked them.

None of the parentbears and olderbears wanted their kidbears to become one of the unhappy "*Uns*," of course. They had heard about the *Uns* in their history books. The *Uns* were bears who were *un*caring, *un*kind, *un*ruly, *un*der-achieving, *un*true, *un*happy, and *un*fulfilled.

None of the bears had even imagined there could ever be any *Uns* on Excellence. Not until now, that is. Now, for the first time, they had seen it for themselves.

Parentbears had noticed that many of the youngerbears were starting to look and act differently than before. It was exactly as though someone had taken the light and the brightness, the *vision,* out of their wonderful young bear eyes. Now, instead of eyes filled with light and life, their eyes looked dull and empty. It was the way youngerbears and kidbears would look if something had stolen their spirits from them. And something *had*.

Even now, while the bears of Excellence began to work together on the plan that the Great Bear had left for them, the sky high above Excellence looked a little grayer every day. It was the grayness of the Nozone layer, beginning to fill up with the spirits of the little bears of Excellence.

Eli had not told the bears of the plan a moment too soon. For many of the little ones, it could already be too late.

Chapter Nine

Self-Talk for Self-Defense

While the other bears began working on the plan Eli had told to them, old Eli himself, along with several of the sciencebears and technobears, was busy elsewhere. They had hidden themselves away in the special Science and Technology cave where any possible invention could be made. From dawn until dark and beyond, Eli and his special team of bears worked tirelessly, hoping to finish their secret project in time.

None of the other bears knew what Eli and the techno-bears were working on. When they asked him what he was doing, and what his secret project was, Eli just smiled hopefully and said, "You'll see . . . you'll see."

Eli did, in fact, have a surprise in store for the bears of Excellence. If his idea worked, Eli thought, he might just be able to bring the strength and courage of the Great Bear back to them now, and just possibly, a new leaderbear, right when they needed him most. But only time would tell if Eli's idea would work.

Meanwhile, the part of The Plan all the other bears in Excellence were hard at work on was the part that had to do with the kidbears themselves.

In the ancient scroll that had been given to Eli, the Great Bear had written out the secrets for a plan of defense against the Negatroids. It was called *"Self-Talk for Self-Defense."*

The plan used a combination of the ancient art of self-defense, and a precise kind of Self-Talk, a discipline like martial arts, using physical forms, along with special words — powerful, almost magical words.

When used together in exactly the right way, these special steps, movements, and forms, along with the exact right words of Self-Talk, held the promise of turning the terrible words of the Negatroids around and stopping them.

"This was the weapon that the Great Bear himself used to fight off the Negatroids that invaded our planet many years ago," Eli told them. "And now it is time to use the 'Self-Talk for Self-Defense' again."

It was true that once, long ago, the Great Bear had taught all of the bears of Excellence how to use Self-Talk—which meant learning how to think things and say things in a totally different way—*good* instead of *bad, positive* instead of *negative.*

It was because of their new kind of Self-Talk that the earlier bears had been able to turn the planet Average into the planet Excellence in the first place. But that was a very long time ago. By now, many bears had stopped thinking about their Self-Talk, and much of what the Great Bear had taught them had been forgotten.

Many years ago, at the time of the Great Bear, every kidbear on the planet had learned all of the special words of Self-Talk, and all of the steps, and the foot motions, and special hand and arm motions that went along with the magic words.

Now, however, exhibitions of little bears using the special words and forms of Self-Talk for Self-Defense were never seen. They had been all but forgotten. And that was, of course, the very reason why the Negatroids had come back. The Bears had begun to forget what had made Excellence *excellent* in the first place.

They had stopped practicing the self-defense *thinking* techniques that kept their self-esteem strong and unbreakable. They had stopped reminding themselves what they *could* do, and had quietly started to slip into the habit of thinking about what they could *not* do. They had stopped practicing having *vision*, and had started once again to start believing in their *limitations* instead of their *unlimited possibilities.*

The parentbears, and even some of the olderbears, had let their defenses down. That was what had allowed the terrible Negatroids to return to the world of Excellence, and begin, one by one, to take the spirits of their children away from them.

Could the once-powerful self-defense of Self-Talk win the fight for them this time? Could they once again learn the steps and special forms and the words of Self-Talk in enough time to protect the spirits of their children that were even now being pulled away? Only time would tell . . . and there was little time left.

Chapter Ten

Self-Talk Boot Camp

The bears worked around the clock. Instead of attending regular school, the youngerbears of Excellence now spent every waking hour of every day in a special kind of boot camp for bears. To prepare for their defense against the Terrible Negatroids, the bears were attending 'Self-Talk for Self-Defense' classes that some of the very old elderbears, those who still remembered how to do it, had quickly set up for them.

On school playgrounds and on rolley fields and in classrooms, and even in the Great Hall, all of the space had been cleared for the special lessons.

Rows of kidbears could be seen everywhere, practicing their Self-Talk for Self-Defense drills. At first, the lines they stood in looked haphazard and undisciplined. During the first practice days, many of the youngerbears could not remember more than a few of the special Self-Talk words and the special steps and forms they were to follow. But day by day, they got better.

Some of the youngerbears seemed to stand out from the others, and seemed to catch on right away. Marathon Bear was always good at sports, and he was a natural at the physical drills. Believer Bear imagined himself as being an ancient master of the art of Self-Talk for Self-Defense, and he stepped right into the role. Theo Bear wasn't big into physical stuff, but he understood the mind stuff—like the Self-Talk part, and he immediately understood the value of the exercises.

Holly Bear, being very smart, did, too. But mostly, she excelled in the exercise because she wanted to show the other bears that these exercises could be, as her brother Shadrack had said, the salvation of Excellence.

Shadrack, himself, had often found himself concerned about what the bears of Excellence would do if anything bad ever came to their planet. Now, when Shadrack went through the Self-Talk drills, he felt he had always known about this. It was as if in some part of his mind, or in his dreams, he had been thinking about and practicing Self-Talk all his life.

Another of Shadrack's friends, the very spirited Popularity Bear, leaped at the chance to join in, just like she leaped at the chance to do anything exciting and fun.

Even Shadrack's best friend Wheely, the little wheelchair bear, joined in the exercises and flew through them with perfect precision, his small wheel chair turning, swiveling, stopping and starting in exact unison with the rest of the bears.

Everywhere you looked, you could see the youngerbears and kidbears practicing, standing so confident and strong, feet apart, one arm extended forward, hand raised in the universal gesture of "stop." Or you would see them in rows, turning like dancers, elbow and arm raised up, warding off or deflecting the blows of invisible words, and shouting out perfect phrases of Self-Talk for Self-Defense.

". . . Step, and then stop! Shout out a phrase of Self-Talk, turn, shout the phrase again, left arm up, wrist to the sky, shout it out one more time! Now step, turn, right arm up, wrist held high, and stop! Plant your feet, flex your knees, cross your arms above you . . . shout the Self-Talk louder now . . ."

Day after day, the practice continued. Soon, the rows of practicing kidbears grew straighter, their motions more in unison, their words of Self-Talk shouted out together in a perfect harmony of little bear voices.

Every step of every form was precise, and every word was in step with every form. Every step the kidbears and the youngerbears were learning moved in perfect harmony with the powerful words of Self-Talk they were learning to shout out loud, and visualize in their wonderful young bear minds:

I can do this! I believe in the best! I believe in myself! Today is my day! Now, especially. I was born to achieve, and nothing less! I am a winning bear of Excellence! I'm glad to be me, I choose to live up to my best, and I choose to win. Nothing can stop me now! I choose to achieve, and I can do this! I always do everything I can do to be the best bear I can be. I can do this! I can do this! **I can do this!**

The kidbears and youngerbears of Excellence were not learning how to fight with fists and blows. This was not a ritual of warriors learning to fight a war of violence or physical strength. The bears of Excellence were, instead, learning a much stronger way to defend themselves against the Negatroids. The self-defense they learned now was the art of Self-Talk in its most powerful form.

If the Great Bear could have been there to see them now, he would have been very proud of them. With the help of Eli and the other olderbears, they might soon be ready to defend the planet Excellence against the invading Negatroids.

* * * * * * * * * * *

As hopeful as it was to see the kidbears training to defend their planet, it was also sad to see, as some of the parentbears knew all too well, that there were a growing number of the youngerbears of Excellence who were not training with the others. They did not take part in the practice sessions, and they would not be helping defend their planet against the Negatroids.

They were the unfortunate *Uns*, the bears whose spirits had already been taken from them. The kidbears who had become *Uns* did little more than wander the streets of Excellence, searching aimlessly for something they had lost, or sitting listlessly on the sidelines, watching with dead, unmoving eyes, *un*certain, *un*caring, and *un*able to do anything to help.

Meanwhile, far above them, at the edge of space, the spirits of the *Uns* shivered in the cold, gray, unending limbo of the Nozone.

Chapter Eleven

The Giant Incredibears

The bears of Excellence had just one more week to go. The big date their Negatroid defense plan called for would be the anniversary of the day the planet Average had first become the planet Excellence, many, many years ago.

On that day, in the planet's distant past, the bears then, with the help of the Great Bear, had rid their planet of all of the Negatroids who had once ruled them. Now the Negatroids were back, and this time the bears of Excellence hoped it would be the time they would defeat them for good. All of the bears' lives and the future of Excellence depended on it.

As the day approached, every bear (except for the growing number of *Uns* whose spirits were captured in the Nozone layer, which was growing larger every day) was preparing for the battle for Excellence.

Every kidbear and youngerbear practiced his or her steps and forms and the Self-Talk words that went along with them. The olderbears and parentbears also practiced the Self-Talk defenses they had so long ago forgotten.

Meanwhile, Eli and his tireless team of technobears worked endless hours to ready Eli's great surprise. What could they be working on in their science and technology laboratories so far underground in their special science cave?

Could it be a super laser beam gun that would zap the Negatroids with a million volts of laser force? No, probably not. That didn't sound anything like old Eli, and it didn't sound anything like anything you would find on the peace-loving planet of Excellence.

Could it be some new kind of spacecraft that would go out into space and attack the Negatroids' giant fleet of ships? That sounded violent.

Could it be a special net that was so big and so strong that it could haul all of the Negatroids away all at once?

The bears didn't know, and all they could do was wonder. But Eli would tell them nothing. The bears simply knew that whatever Eli was working on, it must be something magical; it must be something wonderful. And very soon, now, they would learn for themselves the secret that Eli was preparing for them, and the surprise that Eli was preparing for the Negatroids.

* * * * * * * * * * *

The momentous day arrived with a golden arc of sunlight cresting the horizon, casting the light of hope across the land of the planet Excellence.

As the sun rose, morning found the children of Excellence standing in long rows, at perfect attention, in the middle of Great Bear Stadium, the largest rolley field on Excellence. All of the olderbears and elderbears and teacherbears and parentbears were there too, stationed strategically around their children– –the old guard standing sentry around the new.

This was the day they had all been waiting for, and finally it had come. It was time to send a message back to the Negatroids.

Everyone was ready.

Everyone was silent.

Everyone waited.

Trying not to move at all, even the olderbears looked carefully out of the corners of their eyes to see if anything was happening. But nothing else moved.

The technobears were nowhere to be seen. Eli Bear himself was nowhere in sight. Everyone waited. Everything was still.

And then there was a sound.

None of the bears of Excellence had ever heard a more powerful sound or anything quite like it before. First, they heard the sound just once. It sounded like the deep boom of thunder, but somewhere underground. It was an amazing sound. Maybe something very *good*. Maybe something very *bad*. But for certain, something very *big*.

Whatever it was, it was coming closer! *"It must be the Negatroids, all attacking at once,"* thought the bears, who stood waiting on the field. "What can we do? How can we fight something that sounds that big, and that powerful?" At first, instead of letting fear step in, the bears of Excellence held their ground. But the gigantic sound kept on coming.

And then, suddenly, it stopped.

Every bear eye stared forward, as directly in front of them, the huge hillside walls of the Great Bear Stadium slowly began to part. The giant doors, sliding on huge rails, moved slowly outward.

The sound of their opening was almost as loud and as terrifying as the powerful booming sound that had stopped just moments ago. Every bear on the field peered intently to try and see what lay in the darkness of the hillside cavern.

There was a movement. A flash of color and a reflection of light on something that looked shiny and glistening in the morning sun. And all at once, into the sunlight of Excellence, in perfect unison, slowly and powerfully, stepped the most astonishing sight any bear had ever seen.

Three giant bears, taller than any bear *ever*, moving slowly on great feet of shining steel, stepped from the darkness and into the light of Great Bear Stadium. When they did, pandemonium broke loose.

Whatever they had expected, the good bears of Excellence were not ready for this! Suddenly the perfect lines of standing-at-attention-bears became a mass of bears running wildly, trying to get away. Some were yelling, some were shouting, but most of them were just running, anywhere and everywhere.

Then, just as suddenly, in the midst of all the running and shouting and chaos, they heard the voice of Eli above the crowd. "Stand fast, bears of Excellence! What you see is here to help you!"

Hearing Eli's voice, one by one the bears stopped, and then turned, and then they began to move cautiously forward, toward the place where Eli stood. Behind him, at perfect attention, their golden armor gleaming in the sun, stood three incredible, giant bears.

"These are your new friends," Eli said proudly, his voice very loud and strong. "This is what we have been working on these days and nights, getting ready for this day.

"These bears are *Positronic Incredibears*," he said. "We call them *Positrons* or 'PTs' for short." They are robotic bears who have been created to help us in our battle against the Negatroids," he told them.

Walking over to the first of the Positrons, Eli said, "This is PT1. His name is Polaris." He walked up to the next giant bear. "This is PT2. His name is Ursus. And PT3 here is called Major.

"Together, these three Positrons may be the greatest force we have here on Excellence," Eli said. "The idea to create them came, in part, from the Great Bear himself," he continued. "In the plan from the Great Bear, he said we would need to create a team of positive bears that would be strong enough to defend us against any Negatroid attack. How to do that exactly, he left up to us, and it looks to me that by creating the Positrons, the technobears got the job done."

All of the other bears were watching Eli and the towering Incredibears in stunned amazement. They could hardly believe what stood silently in front of them. The three giant robotic bears were bigger and stronger than anything they had ever seen. And they were friends! They were the secret Eli had been preparing for them. They were like the Great Bear, come to help them when they needed him most.

"Now listen carefully," Eli continued. "You will need to know how special these Positrons are, and what they can do."

Eli now walked closer to one of the giant bears, and stretching out his cane staff to gesture, he began showing the watching bears each of the special capabilities and all of the special equipment the Incredibears possessed.

"Each of the Positrons wears a large, special backpack. It is armor plated, as is the rest of their apparel. In this backpack is contained the Negatroid Alert System. It will pick up and hear any Negatroid negative that is said against you," Eli said. "And it has the ability to send the same words back to the Negatroids, deflect them and make them harmless.

"Attached to the side of each backpack is a very high-powered megaphone. We call it a 'Negahorn.' That is used to amplify the high-powered negative words launched at us by the Negatroids, or any other words the Positrons want to project back at them.

Anytime a Positron hears a single negative word being said to any kidbear, the positron will immediately swing into action, and with the use of this Negahorn, blast the word back at the Negatroid who sent it.

"Next, I want you to notice the special arm guards and wrist bands the Positrons are wearing. These are Negatroid Word Deflection Shields. Any negative word thrown at them can be immediately deflected and thrown aside where it can't harm anyone.

"You'll also see that the Incredibears are wearing what appear to be headphones or earphones. We call them 'Incrediphones.' Those earphones actually turn the Negatroid words, the *bad* words, into the *right* Self-Talk words. That keeps the Incredibears safe from even the strongest Negatroid attack. As long as they have their Incrediphones on and in place, the negative words of the Negatroids cannot get to them.

"Oh, and one more thing. Those devices that look like eye shields. Those are actually Negatroid Visual Imaging Devices. As you know, no one can really quite see a Negatroid. But Positrons *can*. Being invisible is no longer a defense for the Negatroids. Through these eye shields, the Positrons can get a visual on any Negatroid within a thousand yards.

"Through those same special eye shields, the techno team and I have been able to get some computer photographs of actual Negatroids. I don't mind telling you, it's probably a blessing you can't see them. They're worse than even I had imagined."

Eli paused, and then said, "That makes up the Positron's main armament. All of that, along with their chest, body, and leg armor, and the Positrons are as immune to Negatroid attacks as you can get." And then he added, "You can talk to the Positrons, and they can hear you. They may not talk to you like a normal bear, but that's because they're *not* normal bears. They are designed to do two things and two things only. That is to protect *you*—and to defeat the Negatroids."

Eli explained how the special armor the Positrons wore was designed to deflect any negatives from any source, and send them flying back to whoever had sent them.

If you shouted a negative word or phrase at any of the Positrons, your own words would come right back at you—only a hundred times stronger, louder, and more powerful. So if the Negatroids tried to attack Excellence with a barrage of bad, the Positrons would send it back to them, only much stronger.

To say the bears of Excellence were jubilant and excited would be an understatement. They were overwhelmed with what they were seeing. They crowded around and asked questions, and said silly things to the Positrons, trying to make them talk, but during the whole time, the Positrons said nothing. The day now seemed more like a party than a strategic defense plan. Almost everyone was talking and shouting, and feeling happy once again.

Chapter Twelve

The Little Incredibears

Shadrack Bear, who was always a very positive bear, had been watching and listening carefully. But now, instead of celebrating with the rest of the bears, he started calling his closest bearfriends to him.

When they were circled around him, Shadrack began, "We have a lot to thank the Great Bear for. Especially for the idea he gave old Eli to create the Positronic defenderbears. But I sure hope the technobears got it right when they built these giants. I don't know why," he continued, "but I'm not sure I have a positive feeling about this."

Shadrack's friends, Wheely, Holly, Marathon, Believer, Poppy, Scuba, and Theo Bear, listened carefully to what Shadrack had to say. "I think I have the same feeling you do," Holly Bear said. "Me too," said Believer Bear, who could believe almost anything. "Even though I really want to believe that the Positronic bears can defend us and defeat the Negatroids, I'm not sure it will work."

But all of the other bears continued to be jubilant, when much to their surprise, Eli made another announcement.

"There is more," he said. "There is something else we have for you." Now Eli was talking only to the kidbears and the youngerbears.

"We may win our battle against the Negatroids with the help of the Positrons," he said. "Or we could lose it. Only time will tell. We cannot risk losing our Excellence to the Negatroids. We cannot risk losing you, the future bears of this planet, to something that could destroy you one by one. So we have created something else, just for you."

With that, Eli waved his staff toward the huge hillside doorways from which the Positrons had first entered Great Bear Field. All of the bears turned at once to see the team of technobears pushing large carts filled with dozens and dozens of containers. When they reached in and held up what was in the containers, the little bears of Excellence shrieked in delight.

What each of the technobears held up in their hands was an exact, 3-D-printed, duplicate outfit of the special uniforms the giant Positrons wore. Only these duplicate outfits were *little*. They were Incredibear "outfits" for the kidbears and the youngerbears of Excellence!

The young bears rushed toward the carts with the cartons of uniforms in them. Shouting and yelling, "Me next," they pushed forward, forming a rough line and waiting as patiently as they could as one by one, the little bears of Excellence were fitted with their own personal Incredibear uniforms.

* * * * * * * * * * *

High above the planet Excellence, the Negatroid leaders No and Low watched what was taking place in the Great Bear Stadium far below.

"I can't believe this!" the evil Low was saying. "Our plan to capture the spirits of the bears of Excellence one little bear at a time was going so well!" he hissed, waving a dark shadowy arm outward toward the dreary, haze-like vapors of the Nozone layer surrounding the spaceship *Neanderthal I.* "Look how many of their little bear spirits we've already stolen from them!"

"But now *this!*" Low groaned, hardly able to believe what he and his brother No were seeing on the viewing screens in front of them. It looked like the little bears of Excellence were *celebrating,* and that was something no Negatroid could take.

"Can't you see?" No hissed back. "Don't you see why they're jubilant, and what they're doing? *They're getting ready to DEFEND themselves!*" he screeched. "They've made some giant bears with defense weapons, and now they're arming all the silly kidbears with all the same kind of stuff!" he complained shrilly.

"Now we won't be able to sneak into the lives of the furry little things and pretend to look like their parents or teachers or friends, and corrupt their little minds with horrible bad things about themselves! I *told* you we should do it my way! I *told* you we should attack their minds with our most terrible weapon," No went on. But you wouldn't listen. Well, my fiendishly ugly brother, I'll bet you're listening now!"

"Well . . ." Low stammered, caught off guard by the compliment about his looks. "Perhaps you were right . . . perhaps there is still time left."

Without another word or hiss, the two Negatroid leaders began to prepare their greatest weapon to use against the unsuspecting bears on the planet's surface below them—*The Giant Voice of Doom.*

"How many bad, dark, horrible words and thoughts should we program into the computer thought chamber of *The Giant Voice of Doom?*" asked Low.

"Fill it till the needle goes into the red," said No. "Use every file of bad thoughts, self-loathing, broken spirits, lack of confidence, self-doubt, and self-destructive, fatalistic disbelief that we have on board.

"Let's give them a good sample of how we really think!" No exclaimed, hardly able to quell the feeling of evil excitement that welled up inside him every time he thought about how bad Negatroids could be. "Let's give them everything we've got!" he said, pushing buttons on the control panel, making the final preparations to unleash the power of *The Giant Voice of Doom.*

As he did so, the vast underside of the starship *Neanderthal I* began to open. Rolling on great dark steel tracks, two massive doors slid outward, revealing the face of the giant weapon that lay within. Finally, the two doors stood open, the great weapon facing downward, above the Great Bear Stadium and the unsuspecting bears of Excellence.

There, hidden in the darkness, high in the sky above them, floated the ship *Neanterthal I*, its weapons bay doors open. And then, descending from the weapons bay, there slowly appeared a gigantic stage-like framework holding the two largest subwoofers in the known universe.

Each of the subwoofers was more than half the size of Great Bear Stadium, and each of them was powered by an onboard room of amplifiers so huge that any one of them would have blown every speaker in a Grateful Dead reunion concert. And now, the two megawatt-sized subwoofers, suspended silently in space, waited for one single button to be pushed on the panel in the control room in the center of the ship.

The glow from the control panel lighted the dark shadowy-like features of Low and No, and it surprised each of them, when, in an unusual show of cooperation, they nodded and decided to push the big button in unison. The button was large, about the size of a Negatroid hand, and lighted with a harsh, mustard green and hideous brown glow. Printed across the face of the button were the words:

"THE GIANT VOICE OF DOOM"

PRESS HERE

Chapter Thirteen

The Giant Voice of Doom

In the stadium below, each of the kidbears had his or her own special backpack and a set of Incrediphones, two special Negatroid Word Deflector arm shields and wristbands, and in place of the armor plating, his or her own uniform T-shirt. Printed on the front of each shirt, in bold, gold lettering, were the words *You are Special!*

No Negatroid would be able to steal their spirits now, they told each other excitedly. Now they felt like they could handle *anything*!

Hurriedly, they began clambering into their outfits, pulling and turning each piece this way and that, trying to get their little arm shields on right side up instead of upside down, their wrist bands on and pointed outward instead of inward, while their special protective earphones still mostly lay on the ground as the kidbears tried to figure out the right way to flip the switches and push the buttons that would turn everything on and get it working right.

But just then, without warning, the Negatroids struck! A powerful wave of darkest despair, filled with a thousand words of doubt and doom, blasted through the stadium and the crowd of bears within it. Suddenly the air was *filled* with every most unimaginable, negative thought and word the bears of Excellence had ever heard—and many words and thoughts they had never heard before.

The first wave of *The Giant Voice of Doom* hit Great Bear Stadium with a sledgehammer of sound. Its huge subwoofers blasted the land below it with a powerful surge of negative thoughts and dread so strong that it cascaded over the field in giant waves of fear and panic, spreading out and rolling through Excellence like a tsunami of angry raging thought, drowning out the good, and leaving only the rubble of broken littlebear minds and thoughts behind it.

And what was even worse, the deep pulsing waves of woe didn't stop. They continued to blast down on the bears—an unrelenting, endless torrent of negatives, a dark, frightening river of words flooding the landscape of Excellence with nothing but doom.

Some of the words the bears didn't even understand, or couldn't make out clearly. Some of the words they could actually hear; they could make them out. And some of the words and messages they could only *feel*, the Negatroids' giant subwoofers in the dark sky above them, pounding and pounding the worst of the thoughts into their precious young minds . . .

"You're not good enough; you won't succeed; you can't win; you're a loser and you always were; you can't be counted on; you never do anything right; you're not smart enough; you're afraid of your own shadow; you'll never

amount to anything; why even try? You'll never have any luck; nobody likes you; why don't you just admit it, you're nobody, you're nothing at all; that's all you'll ever be . . ."

From the moment the attack of the Negatroids began, the bears had been caught off guard. They hadn't even had the time to get their defensive gear put on properly, or learn how to use the shielding, or even put on the Incrediphones that might have stopped the words.

As wave after wave of destructive words and relentless pictures of defeat were driven into their minds, the bears of Excellence began to stumble and fall, clasping their hands to their ears, trying to shut out the overpowering attack of *bad*.

The Bears of Excellence had wanted to do so well. They had been so sure of themselves! But nothing had prepared them for *this*.

"Maybe the Negatroids are right," one little bear cried out as he fell forward to the ground, no longer able to shield his ears from the poisonous programs of words that now blocked every other thought from his mind.

"Let us listen to the Negatroids!" one of the older bears cried out, unable to keep out the wave of negative thoughts and beliefs and ideas that roared like an avalanche of unbelief through his unprepared mind.

The torrent of negatives that poured over the bears of Excellence was merciless. It was a deluge of "wrong," that had such great force that nothing—not anyone or anything—could stop it.

*   *   *   *   *   *   *   *   *   *   *

It was the Negatroids' greatest moment. From far above the field of Great Bear Stadium, the evil No and his equally evil brother Low had seen the little bears gathering. They had watched them as they had assembled in lines, trying to ready themselves for their defense.

They had watched as the old gray-haired bear named Eli had brought forth their only hope and salvation: three robots that did not even speak or do anything to help the little bears below. And the terrible, evil Negatroids had watched as the littlest of the bears had so eagerly put on their little costumes, trying to look like those stupid, unmoving, unspeaking robots who could do nothing at all.

"This was almost too easy," Low smiled a snarling kind of smile to his treacherous brother, No. "I congratulate you, No," he said. "You were right. It was right to attack them now, when they were preparing for their pitiful defense. With our dark and cunning nature, my evil brother, we could not fail."

And with that, both No and Low looked into the viewing screens above their control panel to watch the triumphant victory over the bears of Excellence on the stadium field below them.

* * * * * * * * * * *

Down below, things were very grim. Within minutes of the first negative volley of thundering words from *The Giant Voice of Doom*, the Negatroids appeared to have completely annihilated the once positive attitudes of the bears of Excellence.

By now, many more bears had fallen. Taken by complete surprise, even many of the most positive and strongest of the bears had been struck down by the subwoofers' powerful words of woe. Some bears still stood or ran among the troops, but they, too, held their hands to their ears, trying to keep out the destructive words of the Negatroids' attack. By now, all but the best of them were beginning to falter.

Soon, all would be lost. *All* of the bears of Excellence, not only their children, would be defeated. And with that defeat, their spirits would be frozen forever in the cold, dark space of the Nozone. There, their spirits would float forever, unthinking, unmoving, and unknowing, like the little kidbear spirits who one by one, even now as the battle raged, were gliding silently up into the sky, and were gathering in the frigid haze of the Nozone.

If the battle of words with the terrible Negatroids was lost, those little spirits would never live again. And right now, it looked as though this was one battle that could never be won.

Chapter Fourteen

Positrons in Position

Later—no one really remembered when, exactly—Eli gave the command. Whenever it was, and however it happened, there is no doubt among any of the bears who were there, *what* happened next.

By all accounts, at the precise moment when things were at their worst, the single minute when things could not have been darker, the bears of Excellence heard old Eli shout over the fray. "Positron One, *take position!* Positron Two, *take position!* Positron Three, *take position!*"

There had been a pause, and then Eli spoke again. Right in the midst of the battle for their minds, Eli's voice chimed out clearer and brighter than any bell of liberty the bears of Excellence had ever heard.

And in that one, shining moment, all old Eli said was, "POSITRONS . . . *DEFEND!*"

Never had any of the bears of Excellence seen anything like what happened next. Never, either, had the Negatroids expected what was about to take place.

If there was chaos before, there was discipline now. Right in the midst of the worst wave of negative words that the bears of Excellence had ever heard, all of them heard three very distinct, very loud and powerful, and very welcome sounds.

The first sound was the first step each of the giant Positrons made as they turned perfectly into "DEFEND" position. The second sound was the click of each of the Positrons detaching the large Negaphone from its backpack.

The third sound was a rapid, precision-like, harmonious sound of robots in motion, as the three Positrons turned, threw up their powerful arms with their Negatroid Deflectors clearly in place, raised their heads skyward, and seeing the sound waves of the Giant Voice of Doom continuing to descend upon them, stepped one step forward, and launched the defense of Excellence.

Suddenly the tsunami wave of negative thoughts that had been bombarding the bears slowed, twisted, turned upward, and in a screaming tornado of sound, hurled itself back into the dark sky, aiming itself directly at the Negatroid spaceship *Neanderthal I.*

Traveling at the speed of sound, it took less than a minute for the swirling pulsing wave of *the Negatroids' own words*, now turned *against* them, to reach *Neanderthal I* and the two massive, pounding subwoofers of The Giant Voice of Doom beneath it.

Following an old rule of something the bears knew from school as "elementary physics," the tsunami-like sound waves of words, sent back at them, once they hit the subwoofers, cancelled all of the booming words the Negatroids were sending out. The result was *silence.*

The Giant Voice of Doom was stopped.

After a minute or two of absolute silence from the Negatroids, there was only one final word message that came back down to the bears gathered in the stadium. Those words were: *"That's very good, little bears of Excellence. Now hit us with the worst words you can send us."*

Down on the ground, during the silence, every bear in the stadium was scurrying to get their battle outfits in place, adjusting their arm guards and wristbands to prepare to send every negative word or thought right back to the Negatroids. Finally assembling into perfect ranks, ready to do battle, their headphones in place, their armor on straight, the kidbears and youngerbears got ready for anything that could happen next.

Meanwhile, the great Positrons continued to aim their powerful Negaphones skyward, ready to reverse any possible negative thought or word from the Negatroids, and send it back to the Negatroid ships in the dark sky overhead.

Chapter Fifteen

The Trap

"Wait!" shouted Shadrack Bear, making his way through the mass of assembled kidbears and youngerbears, as he ran toward old Eli. The elderbear stood next to the Positrons, ready to give his next command. *"Wait,"* shouted Shadrack. *"Something is wrong!"*

When he finally made his way to stand in front of old Eli, Shadrack was still shouting, "Wait, every bear wait!"

Eli looked down at Shadrack and asked, "What is it, young Shadrack? Why should the bears wait? They are all ready now."

"Eli, sir," Shadrack said to the old, wise bear Eli. "We *have* to wait," Shadrack said, almost out of breath from running. "Something is *wrong*!"

"What is it?" Eli asked, looking down at Shadrack with a knowing smile in his eyes, for old Eli knew something about Shadrack that had been foretold by the Great Bear. "All the bears of Excellence are finally ready to fight the Negatroids by sending their negative words and thoughts back to them. What do you think is wrong?"

"Eli, sir," Shadrack began, his words shaking a little as he spoke. "Eli, sir, the Positrons were programmed by the technobears to send the Negatroids' own negative words and thoughts back to them. And now all of the bears are prepared to do the same. But if we do that, we will all *lose*," he insisted.

"And why is that?" old Eli asked, with a great twinkle in his eye as he did so.

"Eli, sir," Shadrack began again. "If our Positrons and all of our bears send the same words of hate and negative and anger and fear back to the Negatroids, we will only be doing what they *want* us to do. We have to do the opposite," Shadrack said. "We have to do the *opposite*!"

* * * * * * * * * * *

In the dark, ghost-like spaceship *Neanterthal I*, the evil Low looked across the ship's dimly-lighted control panel at his brother No.

"What a great trap we set," Low said in a chortling wheeze. "They took the bait! The bears of Excellence are standing at the ready to throw every bad word, every negative thought, every evil idea we send to them back to us. How could they know that evil feeds on evil, or that bad words and terrible thoughts are exactly what make bad things stronger?"

"Right you are," the equally evil No hissed back at his Negatroid brother. "Not *one* of those foolish bears down there has the slightest idea that what their simple robots, and all of the real bears with their stupid Negatroid-repellent costumes are about to do, is send us the exact negative words that we feed on, and make us *stronger!*"

No's attempt at a laugh was a gurgling hiss he almost choked on, and caused his brother Low to scowl, which is what Negatroids do instead of smiling. "We have them now!" croaked the evil Low. "All we have to do is fire the *Giant Voice of Doom* one more time, and the bears of Excellence will respond in kind."

With the word "kind," sticking uncomfortably in his throat, Low glanced down at the *The Giant Voice of Doom* button that was labeled, PRESS HERE, and said, "Let's do it now!" he said impatiently. I'm ready to destroy all of them."

And with that, Low prepared to push the button for *The Giant Voice of Doom*, that

would be the death blow for the little bears of
Excellence far below.

Chapter Sixteen

The Shadrack Defense

"Reverse the *polarity*, reverse the *words*," Shadrack shouted to Eli, knowing they had little time to waste or prepare.

"The Negatroids are trying to trick us into sending them what *they* want, what they *live* for," Shadrack said. "They want us to send them the same negative kinds of thoughts and words and ideas that they live by. That's what gives them their *power*," Shadrack shouted. "We have to send them what they *don't* want. We have to send them what they fear most. We have to send them '*us*,'" he finished, almost out of breath.

"Reverse the words we send to them, reverse the polarity," Shadrack shouted again. "We've got to do it *now!*"

Because the bears of Excellence had been practicing for days and nights, working hard at their self-defense forms and their Self-Talk words, in spite of the earlier confusion and the negative onslaught of words and thoughts they had endured, they were ready.

When old Eli spoke to them now, with Shadrack standing at his side, every bear listened, and was ready to do what they needed to do next. Old Eli knew exactly what he was doing, of course, and he smiled proudly as he looked down at young Shadrack. He had waited for this moment for a very long time.

"Reverse the polarity," old Eli shouted out to them. "Change your armbands and shields from 'Receive and Repel,' to 'Send.' Instead of sending the Negatroids' negative words back to them, let's send them the words of Excellence! Let's show them what makes Excellence work." And then, turning to the

three giant Positrons, Eli said, "Reverse polarity. Send the *good*."

When the next tidal wave of negative thoughts and words powered their way through the once colorful skies of Excellence, and hit the bears, standing in perfect formation below, the evil brothers Low and No thought that every single bear on the field would do nothing more than send their own negative, malicious thoughts back to them, feeding their own need for "bad."

But they were wrong.

Every word and thought of *The Giant Voice of Doom* tsunami from the great subwoofers of *Neanderthal I* that cascaded downward toward Excellence was met with a very different kind of defense. Instead of *warfare*, the Negatroids were met with an onslaught of *peacefare.*

Every word and thought from the Negatroids was met with a deluge of thousands more words of *"good"*— *positive attitude, creativity, self-belief, self-confidence, joy, sharing,* and a huge amount of something the Negatroids had never been able to defeat— —the word and feeling called *"love."*

During the battle of "good and evil," that was being waged on the planet Excellence, every bear had gotten the message, and they now knew what to do. Word for word, thought for thought, the bears of Excellence fought a war, not of arms and armament, but a war of ideals, belief, and growth.

The Terrible Negatroids who were waging an all-out war against the planet Excellence *hated* good. They hated positiveness. They hated personal growth, and good attitudes of any kind. And now, from the bears of Excellence, the Negatroids were being bombarded with good. Good was awful, it was un*bear*able. But like a lot of bad people, even with a lot of good words and thoughts surrounding them, the Negatroids refused to stop.

At one point during the battle, Eli shouted to Shadrack, who was, by then, sending every positive, self-believing message he could, skyward toward the Negatroids. *"Push the button,"* the old bear yelled to Shadrack above the deafening clash of good words against bad. *"Push the gold button!"*

Chapter Seventeen

The Winning Sky

The new volley of the Negatroids' tsunami of negative words and thoughts had not taken the bears of Excellence by surprise like the first attack had. Now, with the new, totally positive words of Excellence, this time they had stood their ground.

Still shouting his most powerful positive thoughts to ward off the monstrous word attack of *The Giant Voice of Doom*, Shadrack had stumbled a time or two, but he had not fallen. With the words of Eli bear still ringing in his ears, Shadrack kept going. "Push the button! *Push the gold button!*" old Eli had shouted to him across the din of battle and the field of bears.

But *what* gold button had he meant? Shadrack had pushed every button on his anti-Negatroid arm shields and his wrist bands, but none of them had seemed to make any difference. The Negatroids had kept coming, and their *Giant Voice of Doom* subwoofers in the sky had already sent a third wave of negative blasts that were, even now, being countered by the brave little protectorbears on the rolley field below.

Shadrack pushed his ear protectors even tighter over his young bear ears and tried to think. "Even with our positive words, the Negatroids aren't going to give up easily," he thought. And then he thought about Eli's words again. "*Push the gold button,*" Eli had shouted.

"What gold button?" Shadrack thought, thinking as hard as he could think.

"Okay," he thought. "I have buttons on my anti-Negatroid outfit, but I've pushed all of them, and it didn't do anything extra. There must be some other button I can push." And then, thinking even harder, Shadrack thought about every button he had ever seen. "Where is there another button I could push?" he thought. "What is the gold button Eli was shouting about?"

It might have come from his training to think well, or it could have come from his sense of self—the kind of thinking he was taught over the years during his positive attitude training on Excellence. But from somewhere, Shadrack thought about the time his father had taken him to see the place in Great Hall where, on that special occasion, his father had been privileged to push a button to start a celebration.

"Great Hall," Shadrack thought. *"There are buttons in Great Hall!"*

With that thought, Shadrack quickly began to make his way through the throng of youngerbears and olderbears, still sending super-positive messages in response to the latest wave of negatives from the Negatroids' *Giant Voice of Doom*, and found his way to Great Hall.

Once inside, the din of the word battle outside lessened somewhat. Remembering the day his own father had taken him there, now, making only one wrong turn, Shadrack carefully made his way to the room where he had seen a control panel with all kinds of holovision screens, and most certainly—and he could see it clearly in his mind—*a row of buttons.*

And then, there it was. Right in front of him. A desktop panel with 12 lighted buttons——all of the buttons for the 12 greatest celebrations on Excellence.

Most of them were about the size of one bearpaw finger. And they had words printed above them. *"Graduation,"* said one. *"Winning Rolley"* was printed above another. *"New Births,"* said another. Above another it read, *"Anniversaries."* And at the far right end of the 12 buttons, there was one, very large, brightly-lighted gold button that read,

"Great Bear Day Super Celebration."

Shadrack looked at the panel of lighted buttons with awe. These were the launch buttons for all of the skyrocket fireworks displays for all of the great celebration days of Excellence!

And here was the button Eli had wanted him to press, the one celebration button that might help them now.

"It's the 'Great Bear Super Celebration' button," he thought. "That will send dozens of exploding colorful skyrockets, and tons of lighted-up positive messages into the sky over Excellence, and that will surely stop the Negatroids with a celebration of 'good!' So that has to be the button old Eli wants me to press," Shadrack said out loud to himself. "'*The Great Bear Day Super Celebration*' button.'"

But just as he said the words, a thunderous volley of new, negative thoughts and words erupted from the next wave from the Negatroid's *Giant Voice of Doom*, and Shadrack was thrown to the floor as the windows of the Great Bear control center blew inward, showering the room with glass, and upending the control panel with the button he had been about to press.

"I can do this," Shadrack said, in perfectly controlled cadence of mind and thought. "I can do this," he repeated again. "I can do this!"

Picking himself up from the floor, shaking the pieces of broken glass and computer parts that clung to his fur, Shadrack stood up, tall and straight, and looked down at the mangled control panel with the 12 lighted buttons that still glowed in front of him.

"Press the button," he said again, shaking the fog of Negatroid attack words from his mind, remembering again the last thing that old Eli had shouted to him. *"Press the gold button."*

And then, standing tall, as a leader should, Shadrack reached forward to the still lighted fragment of control panel in front of him. He smiled slightly, nodded his head, and said the words, *"I can do this."* And just when it mattered most, Shadrack made a decision.

In one precise moment, instead of pressing just one button, Shadrack pressed *all twelve of them.*

* * * * * * * * * * *

No one who was there on the planet Excellence that night would ever forget what happened next.

In that moment, when Shadrack pushed the twelve buttons, the skies of Excellence erupted in a cacophony of sound and an explosion of fireworks of light and brilliance that had never been heard or seen before. The sky above Excellence suddenly erupted into the most brilliant display of positive light and messages that any world would hope to receive.

Rocket after rocket catapulted into the sky with dazzling star-spangled messages of sparkling, bright, shimmering light that read, *"You Are a Winner," "You Can Do It," "I*

Believe in You!" "You Are Exceptional!" "Congratulations!" "You're the Best!" "The Great Bear Lives!" and *"Love Rules!"*

The rockets and fireworks with their messages of belief and love and congratulations went on and on without letup. Flares and rockets and a sky filled with explosions of light of every color turned the night sky of Excellence almost into daylight. Because Shadrack had pushed *all* of the celebration buttons, instead of just one of them, far into the night the entire sky above Excellence exploded, again and again and again, with the dazzling messages of positive.

The winning sky of Excellence was a show of *positive* that no negative—and no Negatroid—could endure.

The next morning, when daylight finally returned, the dark armada of Negatroid ships was gone.

Chapter Eighteen

The Spirits of the Nozone

It was early dawn the next morning, after the Negatroids had gone, and while most of the bears of Excellence were finally settling down after celebrating and rejoicing, that Shadrack noticed something unusual.

What had been a cold, frozen layer of haze over the planet was changing.

"Something is happening," Shadrack shouted to the other bears. Old Eli, standing nearby, looked upward as the sky began to change. Soon, all of the bears of Excellence were looking skyward, to watch.

From somewhere high above them, something amazing was happening. It was like they were seeing stardust, as brilliant sparkles of light began to descend from the sky.

First the bright, twinkling lights of stardust were formless, just little golden star-fragments of beautiful light, drifting and swooping downward. And then, the sparkles of golden light began to take on the embryo-like, gossamer form of beautiful shining little bears.

And almost as though they had minds of their own, the shimmering, shining little bear stars began swooping down, one by one, until finally, each of them very carefully and lovingly touched a little bear of Excellence.

Each of the bears the bright stars of light were touching was one of the *Uns*, the bears whose spirits had been stolen and locked away in the Nozone.

And now, as Shadrack and his friends, and all the motherbears and fatherbears of

Excellence watched in awe, the littlebear spirits that had been stolen away were finding their way home to the bears who had lost them.

As they watched, each bear who had lost its spirit began to shake its little bear head, like it was waking up from a very long, deep slumber, and began to come to life again.

Sparkling light by sparkling light, the bright, shining spirits from the Nozone found each of the bears who had lost them. Their spirits had been set free, and all of the troubled little *Uns* were complete, wonderful little bears once again.

Their spirits had come home.

Chapter Nineteen

Epilogue

The night the Negatroids left, driven back into space by the incredible show of positive by the bears of Excellence, the evil Low had looked across the control room's view screens on the spaceship *Neanderthal I*. "This isn't fun anymore," he hissed at his brother No.

"They've beaten us, then?" No asked.

"I wouldn't say *that*," Low breathed back at him, trying to pretend they had not just been soundly beaten. "I just hate happy things. And I hate fun things. And I hate positive things. And most of all, I hate bears. And *fireworks*!"

Then his gaze grew distant, his evil, glowing slits of eyes imagining something far away. "I suggest a change of plans."

Carefully studying his galaxy maps, only one thought was on Low's mind, and that was the need to find an easier planet to attack next—one without so much positive. Determined to not let their defeat on Excellence put an end to their planet-killing chaos, the evil Low scanned the great starlists of susceptible planetary systems until he found one planet that looked just right.

"I have one," Low suddenly screeched to his brother. "It is the *perfect* planet for us to attack next! It has an odd name, but it looks like exactly the right kind of planet for us."

Then, studying the data file more closely, Low did his best to rub his shadowy, ghostlike Negatroid hands together and said, "We're in luck! It's a planet that's already in trouble! It is overrun with wars. It is filled with prejudice, people killing each other in the streets, drug problems, gadget worship, and troubled kids.

"It's perfect! We will destroy any hope they have left, fill their minds with darkness, freeze their children's spirits in the Nozone, and doom their precious little planet forever."

Low then carefully typed the few strokes of one short command onto the control screen in front of him.

And with that, he paused, one scrawny, shadowy finger poised over a large button on the instrument panel. He looked up, just for a moment, trying to hide the feeling of excitement that was growing inside him as he caught his brother's gaze. It was a look that was exactly mirrored in the eyes of his evil brother No.

They did *so* love to find a new planet to destroy!

Low grimaced his version of a smile. And then he looked down at the button. It read:

EXECUTE

"We're out of here!" he screeched, and pushed the button.

In a single moment, the spaceship *Neanderthal I* and its huge armada of shadowy, ghost-like Negaships left the constellation Ursa Major.

In that same moment, the entire dark fleet of Negatroid ships reappeared in a different sky of stars far away from Excellence, and emerged over a small, beautiful green and blue planet.

It was the planet called "Earth."

The End

Shadrack will return in

The Incredibears on Planet Earth

www.SelfTalkPlus.com

For information:

Dr. Shad Helmstetter
www.shadhelmstetter.com

Self-Talk Audio Programs
www.SelfTalkPlus.com

Self-Talk Training
www.selftalkinstitute.com

Life Coach Training
www.lifecoachinstitute.com

Made in the USA
Columbia, SC
22 December 2018